W9-CDJ-033

Each illustration in this
book is watercolor and pencil.

First U.S. edition 1996.
Printed in Hong Kong.
Published in the
United States by
Little Friend Press,
Scituate, Massachusetts.

ISBN 0-9641285-4-3

Library of Congress
Catalog Card Number: 96-075796

Second Printing

LITTLE FRIEND PRESS

28 NEW DRIFTWAY

SCITUATE, MASSACHUSETTS 02066

In memory of Peter Francis Amiss
who knew Heaven on earth and now
lives in Heaven and in our hearts.

*"In all thy ways acknowledge him, and
he shall direct thy paths."*

PROVERBS 3:6

*To Jack, Taylor and Barrett, for
helping keep my path lit.*

Heavensbee

2013
Aidan,
May all your dreams come true!

Written by L. A. Murphy

Illustrations by Ronnie Rooney

LITTLE FRIEND PRESS

SCITUATE, MASSACHUSETTS

Have you ever seen a cow
jumping over the moon while
dancing to a rock 'n' roll tune?

Have you ever seen a horse fly a kite
then climb a tree with all his might?

Have you ever seen
an elephant in a bikini
at the beach doing
the swahini?

Well, you see,
there's a place called
Heavensbee,
where anything you
wish or can imagine...
will come true.

HOME
AWAY

Just close your eyes and picture it...

A cat with a bat and a baseball mitt
or a dog at home plate who hits a pop fly,
and an octopus with eight gloves
who lets it get by!

Have you ever seen a cat chase a dog
or a mosquito catch a frog?

Well I have, in Heavensbee.
Heavensbee is a place where
anything can be.

A tree can walk
and a tree can talk.
A chicken can fly
and a fish can cry.

All these things can be
wait and see…
when you imagine them with me.

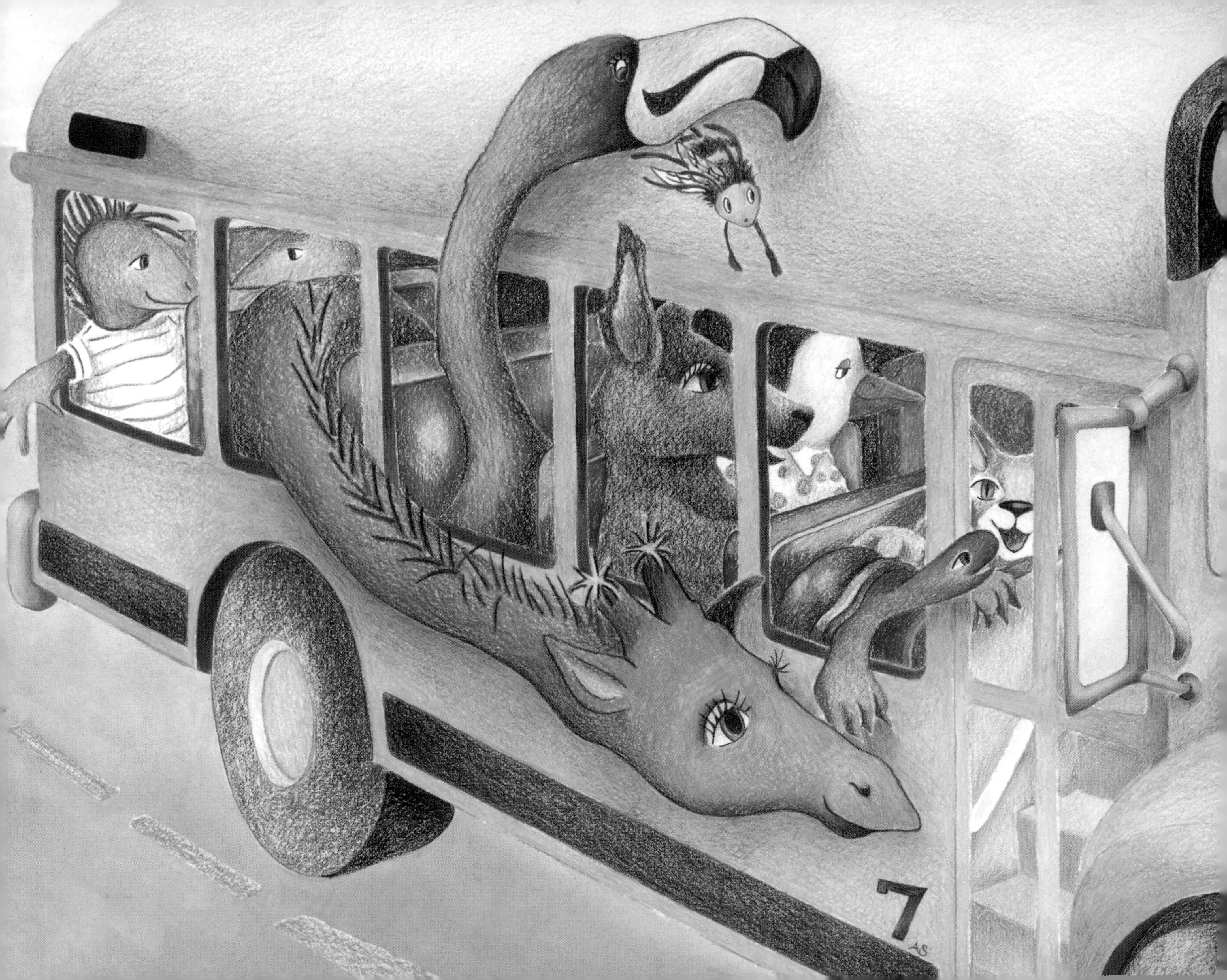
7

Just imagine you and me
riding on a bus
driven by a flea.

Just imagine me and you
in the pouch of a kangaroo.

Where you say?
In Heavensbee,
where anything can be
what it wants to be.

Just use your imagination
and you will see
many things you thought
could never be.

Imagine a crocodile
making friends with your cat,
and going to school
wearing his hat!

Just think of it . . .
we could ski all day
and shoosh,

shoosh,

shoosh away!

Have you ever seen an ant
ride a bike?
It can be . . .
if you like.

Have you ever seen a zebra with polka dots
with the colors of a rainbow for his spots?

Well I have, in Heavensbee
where anything can be
what you want it to be
you shall see.

Imagine a great
dinosaur for your pet
and bringing
him to the beach
to get a little wet!

Imagine your friends
when they see you
at the shore
floating on your
pet dinosaur!

Just remember anything can be . . .

when you imagine it you will see.

I think I will go now
and let you be
to your own imagination
that is bigger than the sea!